This book is **mine** and my name is:

....

....

I REALLY want to SHARE!

Simon Philip

Lucia Gaggiotti

templar
books

One morning, as I lazed in bed,
my parents, smiling, came and said,
"Come snuggle up with us instead.
We've got big news to share."

That's when I learned that we, a three,
a perfect little family,
would soon be four, Mum telling me,
"You'll have to learn to share."

"That's **fine!**" I said. "I cannot wait
to be a sister – I'll be **great!**
Don't worry, I appreciate . . .

It's only
RIGHT
to share!"

At school I let my classmates know
that **everyone** should have their go.

It's *crucial* turns are taken, so
they learn it's nice to share.

It's why for birthday do's I send
all kids an invite to attend.
I'm *such* a thoughtful, selfless friend,
who knows just how to share.

But at my party, suddenly
the focus isn't **all** on me!
I stamp my foot! How **can** this be?

I do not want to share.

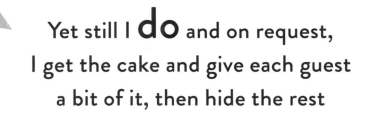

Yet still I **do** and on request,
I get the cake and give each guest
a bit of it, then hide the rest

because I want **my** share.

But when they find my secret spot
and see me gobble down the lot,
they seem upset at what they got,
and say, "You ate our share!"

My parents say, "That **wasn't** right!"
And in my bedroom late that night,
I realise, perhaps I might
not **quite** know how to share . . .

Next day, I'm quickly whisked away
to Gran and Grandad's house, to stay.
They say the baby's due – today!
But what if I can't share?

Then Grandad notices that I
am not myself, and asks me why.
"I always mess things up," I cry,
"because I cannot share."

He smiles and says, "It can be tough
to have to share your favourite stuff.
My guess is you've not trained enough –
one has to **learn** to share."

"I've had to **learn** to share my life . . .
My food . . . my duvet . . . with my wife.

I love her, but it's caused some strife.
It takes a lot to share."

My grandma winks, her smile agleam.
"He sometimes makes me want to scream!

We're only such a super team
because we've learned to share."

So then *I* share my biggest fear:
that when the brand new baby's here,
I'll wreck things, as I've nowhere near
perfected how to share.

I'm scared my parents won't adore
me quite the way they did before.
They might not love me anymore
or have love left to share.

They hug me tight. They comfort me,
and say, "That's **not** how things will be.
They'll love you for eternity!
There's **always** love to share."

And when my brother's born, I'm sure
I've never felt so **thrilled** before.

We
SNUGGLE
and I just
ADORE
the moment
that WE
SHARE!

And now I cannot wait to see
what things we'll do, just him and me!

I'm pretty certain it will be
a lot of fun to share.

But **uh-oh!** All he does is cry,
make horrid smells and occupy

my mum and dad, and that is why
they have no time to share.

And now I'm not so sure I'm glad
my brother's here, as I feel sad.

My mum's exhausted, so is Dad.
They're **way** too tired to share.

But when – **again** – he starts to cry
and nobody can work out why,
or how to make him stop . . . *I* **try**.

I choose something to share.

And, to my **shock** . . .

. . . it works a **treat**!

And suddenly he's just **SO** sweet,
my heart might burst with every beat!
I'm pleased I chose to share.

I'm really glad our family
now totals four – and not just three!
My parents say they're proud of me,
and how I've learned to share.

And guess what? Sharing's **not** so tough.
It happens easily enough,
because there's simply tons of stuff
that feels so **good** to share.

Like cuddles, tickles, secrets, laughs,
my pet, my books, my bubble baths,

my fondest toys and photographs.
I really **want** to share.

And when, again, my birthday comes,
I make amends with all my chums . . .
I give them cake – and **not** just crumbs!

I REALLY love to share!

For Katie Haworth, with huge thanks! x
SP
To my beloved brother Marco
LG

A TEMPLAR BOOK

First published in the UK in 2022 by Templar Books,
an imprint of Bonnier Books UK,
4th Floor, Victoria House
Bloomsbury Square, London WC1B 4DA
Owned by Bonnier Books
Sveavägen 56, Stockholm, Sweden
www.bonnierbooks.co.uk

Text copyright © 2022 by Simon Philip
Illustration copyright © 2022 by Lucia Gaggiotti
Design copyright © 2022 by Templar Books

1 3 5 7 9 10 8 6 4 2

ISBN 978-1-80078-172-6

This book was typeset in Brandon Grotesque
The illustrations were created with collage and digital medium

Edited by Alison Ritchie
Designed by Genevieve Webster
Production by Emma Kidd

Printed in China

FSC
www.fsc.org

MIX
Paper from
responsible sources
FSC® C104723